STAR WARS®

DARTH VADER AND THE LOST COMMAND

VOLUME TWO

SCRIPT
HADEN BLACKMAN

PENCILS
RICK LEONARDI

INKS
DANIEL GREEN

COLORS
WES DZIOBA

LETTERING
MICHAEL HEISLER

COVER ART
TSUNEO SANDA

It is still the early days of the Empire, and Emperor Palpatine's apprentice Darth Vader is still being tested and evaluated by his master—and others. Alone with his own doubts, Vader wonders if he made the right choice in betraying the Jedi and becoming a Sith.

Vader's latest task has brought him to the little-explored Ghost Nebula—specifically, the Atoan system—where Moff Tarkin's son, an admiral for the Imperial fleet, disappeared along with his command months prior.

Believing Admiral Tarkin to be a prisoner of the local inhabitants, Vader and battalions of the 501st Stormtrooper Legion attack and conquer the locals. But then Vader encounters Lady Saro, the system's religious leader . . .

The events in this story take place approximately nineteen years before the Battle of Yavin.

DARK HORSE COMICS

Spotlight

visit us at www.abdopublishing.com

Reinforced library bound edition published in 2012 by Spotlight,
a division of the ABDO Group, PO Box 398166, Minneapolis, MN 55439.
Spotlight produces high-quality reinforced library bound editions for schools and
libraries. Published by agreement with Dark Horse Comics, Inc., and Lucasfilm Ltd.

Printed in the United States of America, North Mankato, Minnesota.
102011
012012
 This book contains at least 10% recycled materials.

Star Wars: Darth Vader and the Lost Command.
Star Wars © 2011 by Lucasfilm, Ltd. and TM. All rights reserved.
Used under authorization. Text and illustrations © 2011 by Lucasfilm, Ltd.
All other material © 2011 by Dark Horse Comics, Inc.

Library of Congress Cataloging-in-Publication Data

Blackman, W. Haden.
  Star wars : Darth Vader and the lost command / script, Haden Blackman ;
pencils, Rick Leonardi. -- Reinforced library bound ed.
      p. cm.
  ISBN 978-1-59961-980-4 (volume 1) -- ISBN 978-1-59961-981-1 (volume 2) --
ISBN 978-1-59961-982-8 (volume 3) -- ISBN 978-1-59961-983-5 (volume 4) --
ISBN 978-1-59961-984-2 (volume 5)
  1. Graphic novels. 2. Science fiction. I. Leonardi, Rick. II. Title.
  PZ7.7.B555Ssm 2012
  741.5'973--dc23

                                        2011033322

All Spotlight books are reinforced library binding
and manufactured in the United States of America.

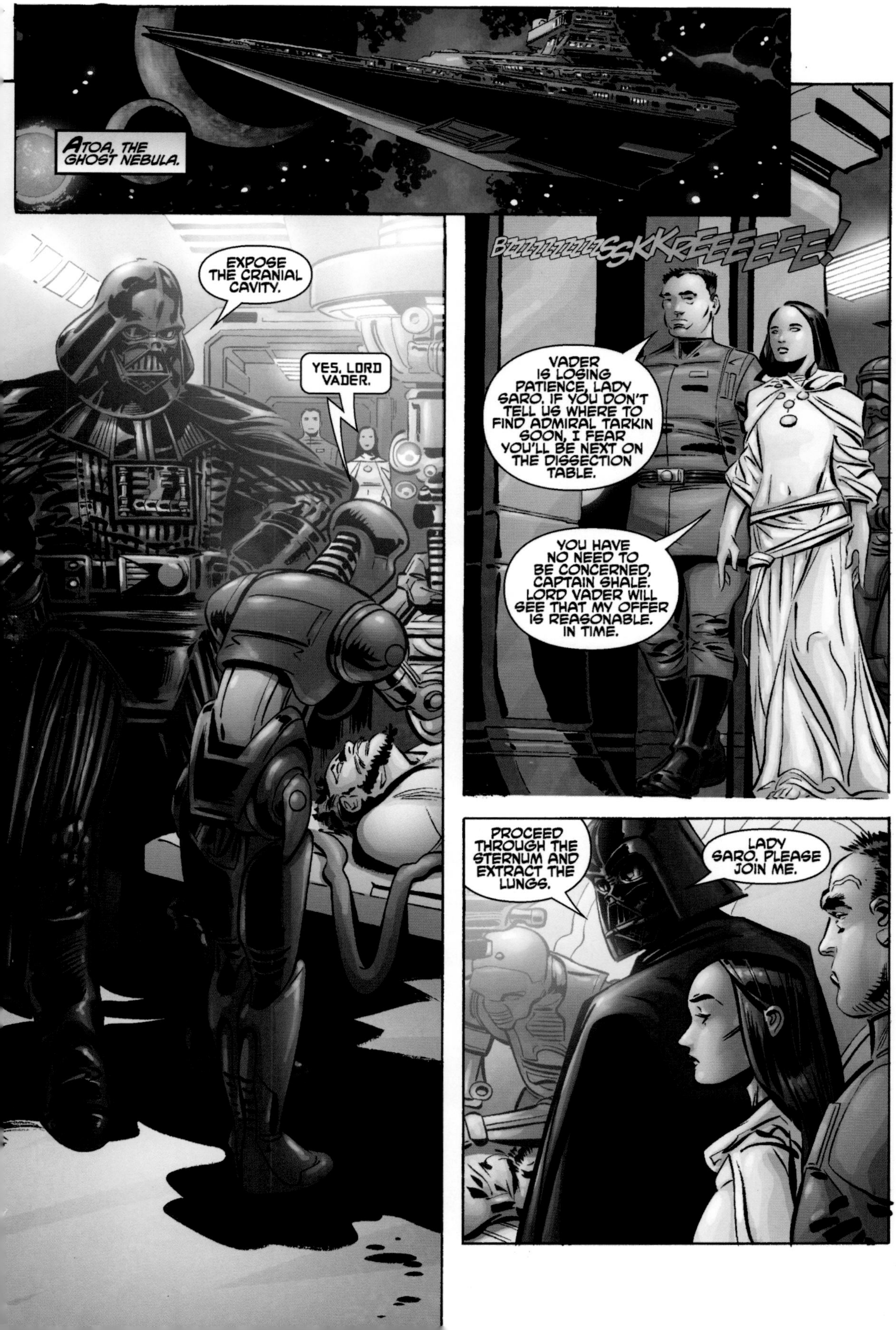
ATOA, THE GHOST NEBULA.
EXPOSE THE CRANIAL CAVITY.
YES, LORD VADER.
BZZZZZZZZZSSKKREEEEEEE!
VADER IS LOSING PATIENCE, LADY SARO. IF YOU DON'T TELL US WHERE TO FIND ADMIRAL TARKIN SOON, I FEAR YOU'LL BE NEXT ON THE DISSECTION TABLE.
YOU HAVE NO NEED TO BE CONCERNED, CAPTAIN SHALE. LORD VADER WILL SEE THAT MY OFFER IS REASONABLE. IN TIME.
PROCEED THROUGH THE STERNUM AND EXTRACT THE LUNGS.
LADY SARO. PLEASE JOIN ME.

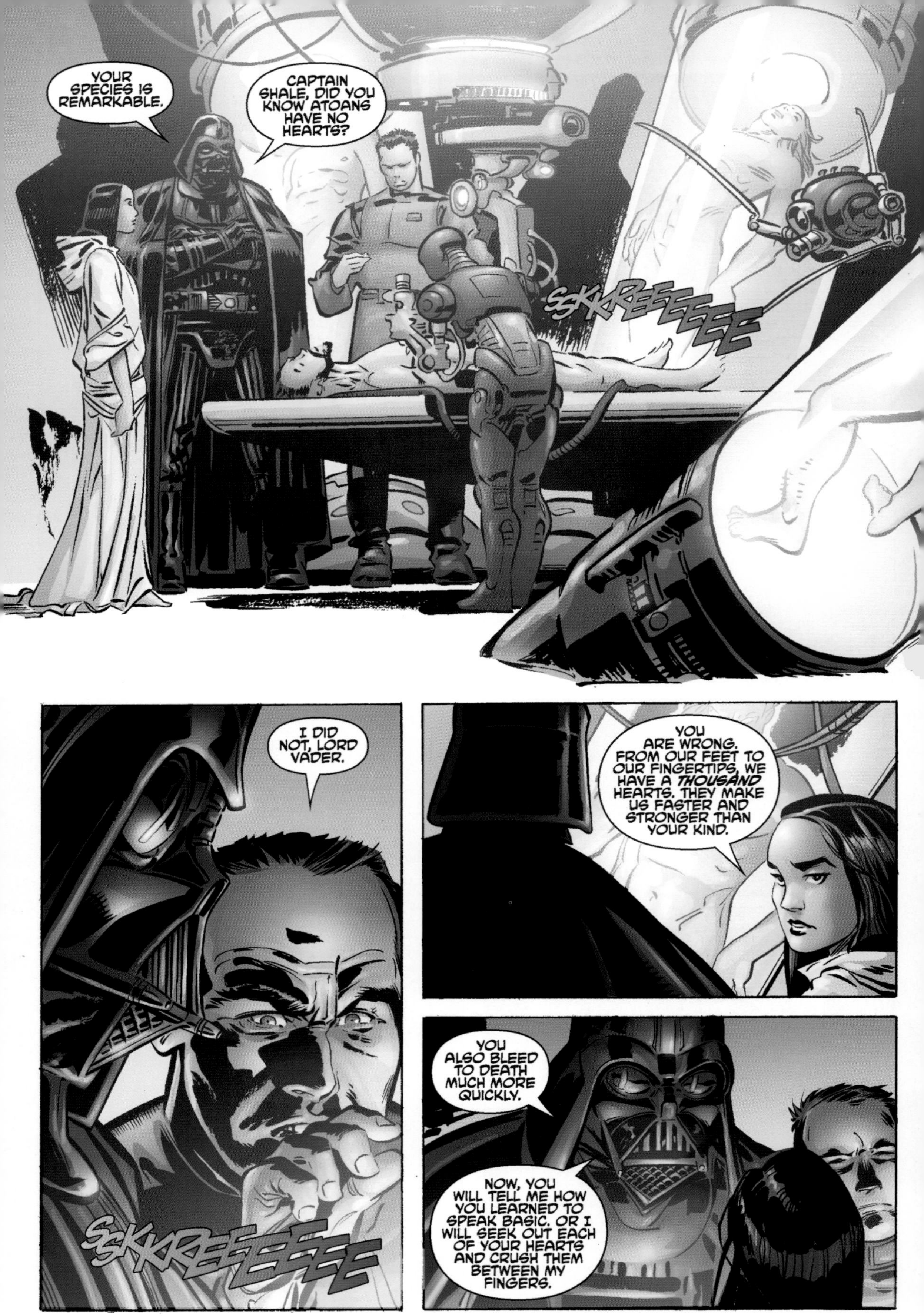
YOUR SPECIES IS REMARKABLE.
CAPTAIN SHALE, DID YOU KNOW ATOANS HAVE NO HEARTS?
SSKKREEEEEEEEE
I DID NOT, LORD VADER.
SSKKREEEEEEEEE
YOU ARE WRONG. FROM OUR FEET TO OUR FINGERTIPS, WE HAVE A *THOUSAND* HEARTS. THEY MAKE US FASTER AND STRONGER THAN YOUR KIND.
YOU ALSO BLEED TO DEATH MUCH MORE QUICKLY.
NOW, YOU WILL TELL ME HOW YOU LEARNED TO SPEAK BASIC. OR I WILL SEEK OUT EACH OF YOUR HEARTS AND CRUSH THEM BETWEEN MY FINGERS.

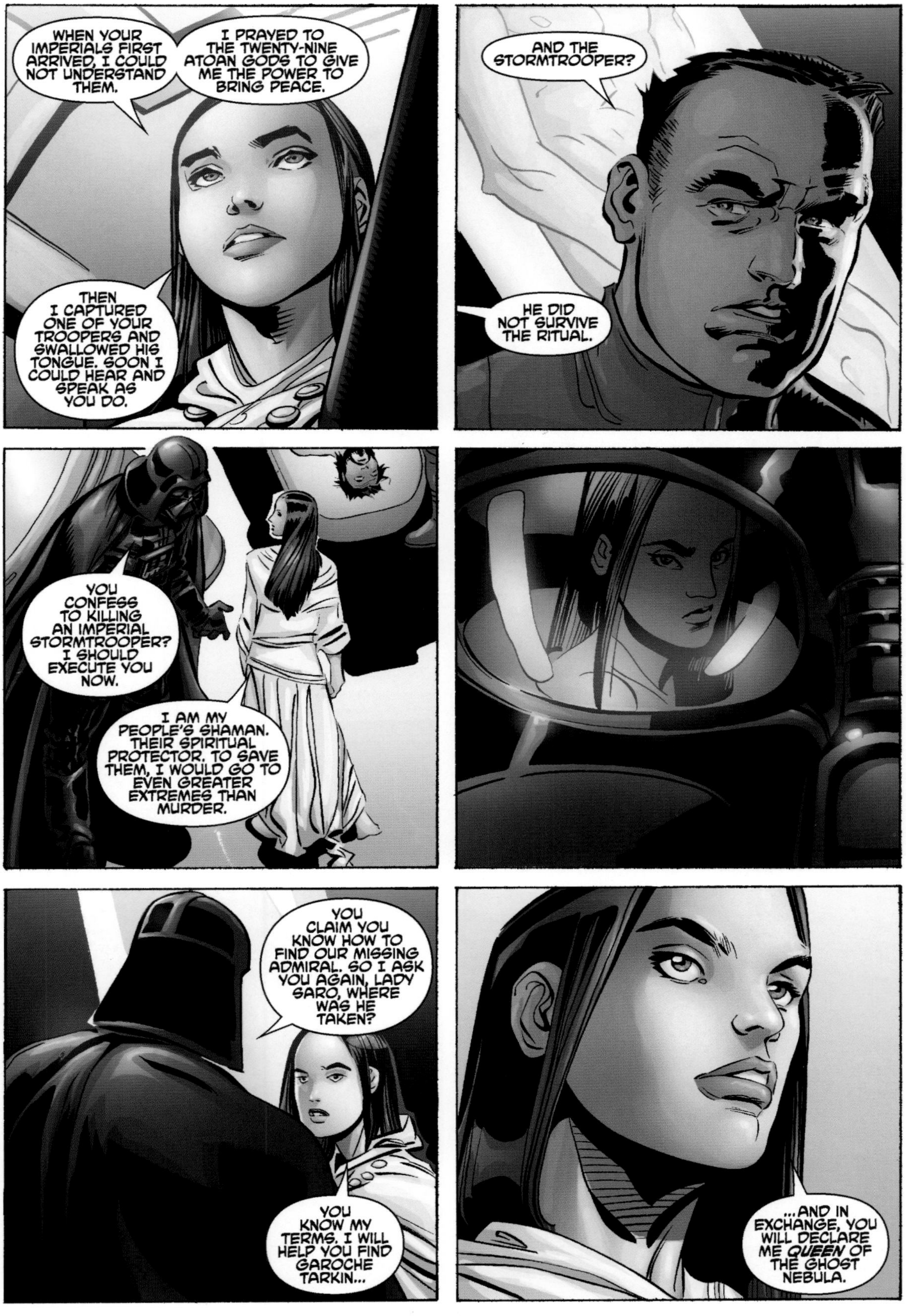
WHEN YOUR IMPERIALS FIRST ARRIVED, I COULD NOT UNDERSTAND THEM.
I PRAYED TO THE TWENTY-NINE ATOAN GODS TO GIVE ME THE POWER TO BRING PEACE.
THEN I CAPTURED ONE OF YOUR TROOPERS AND SWALLOWED HIS TONGUE. SOON I COULD HEAR AND SPEAK AS YOU DO.
AND THE STORMTROOPER?
HE DID NOT SURVIVE THE RITUAL.
YOU CONFESS TO KILLING AN IMPERIAL STORMTROOPER? I SHOULD EXECUTE YOU NOW.
I AM MY PEOPLE'S SHAMAN. THEIR SPIRITUAL PROTECTOR. TO SAVE THEM, I WOULD GO TO EVEN GREATER EXTREMES THAN MURDER.
YOU CLAIM YOU KNOW HOW TO FIND OUR MISSING ADMIRAL. SO I ASK YOU AGAIN, LADY SARO, WHERE WAS HE TAKEN?
YOU KNOW MY TERMS. I WILL HELP YOU FIND GAROCHE TARKIN...
...AND IN EXCHANGE, YOU WILL DECLARE ME *QUEEN* OF THE GHOST NEBULA.

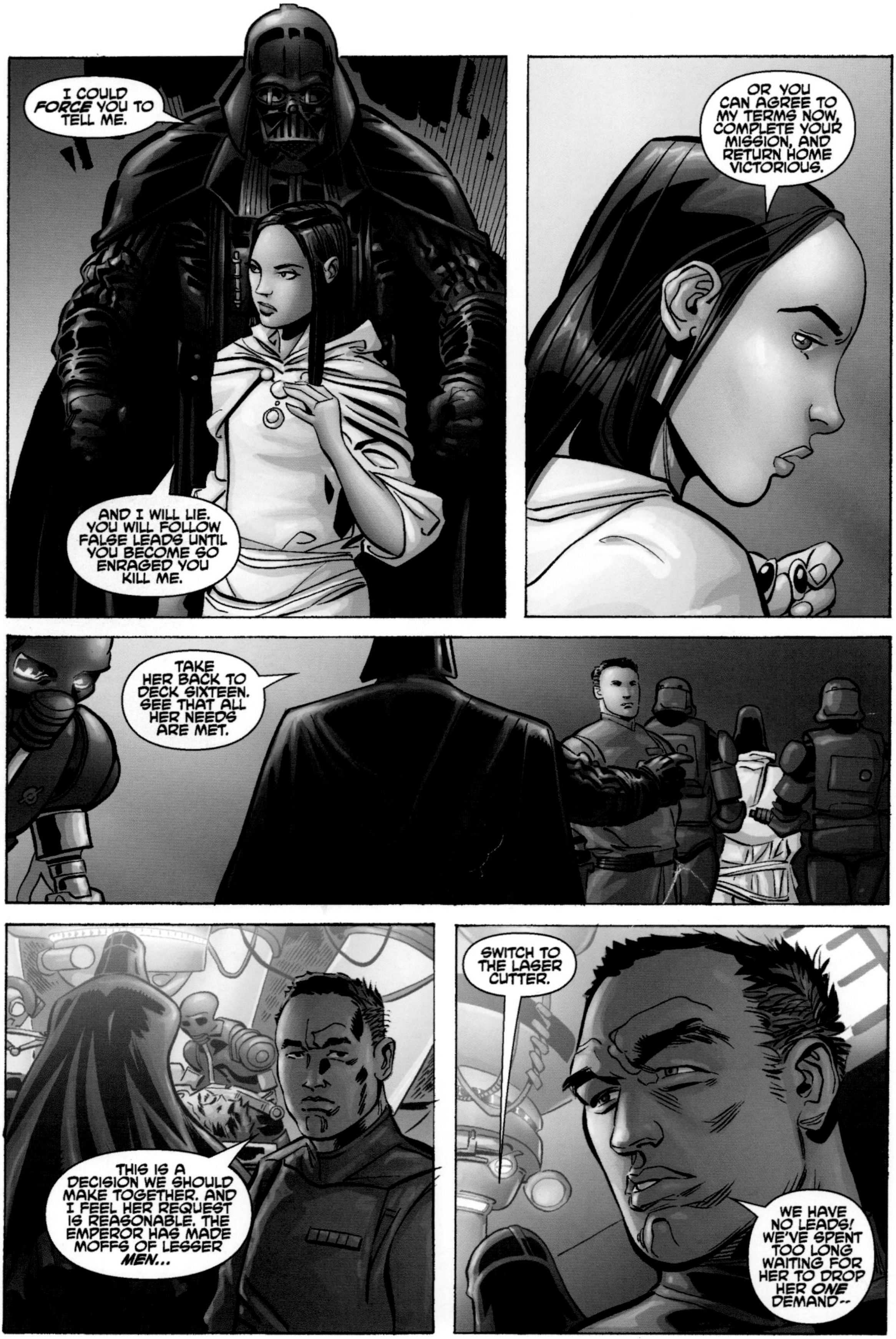

I COULD FORCE YOU TO TELL ME.
AND I WILL LIE. YOU WILL FOLLOW FALSE LEADS UNTIL YOU BECOME SO ENRAGED YOU KILL ME.
OR YOU CAN AGREE TO MY TERMS NOW, COMPLETE YOUR MISSION, AND RETURN HOME VICTORIOUS.
TAKE HER BACK TO DECK SIXTEEN. SEE THAT ALL HER NEEDS ARE MET.
THIS IS A DECISION WE SHOULD MAKE TOGETHER. AND I FEEL HER REQUEST IS REASONABLE. THE EMPEROR HAS MADE MOFFS OF LESSER MEN...
SWITCH TO THE LASER CUTTER.
WE HAVE NO LEADS! WE'VE SPENT TOO LONG WAITING FOR HER TO DROP HER ONE DEMAND--

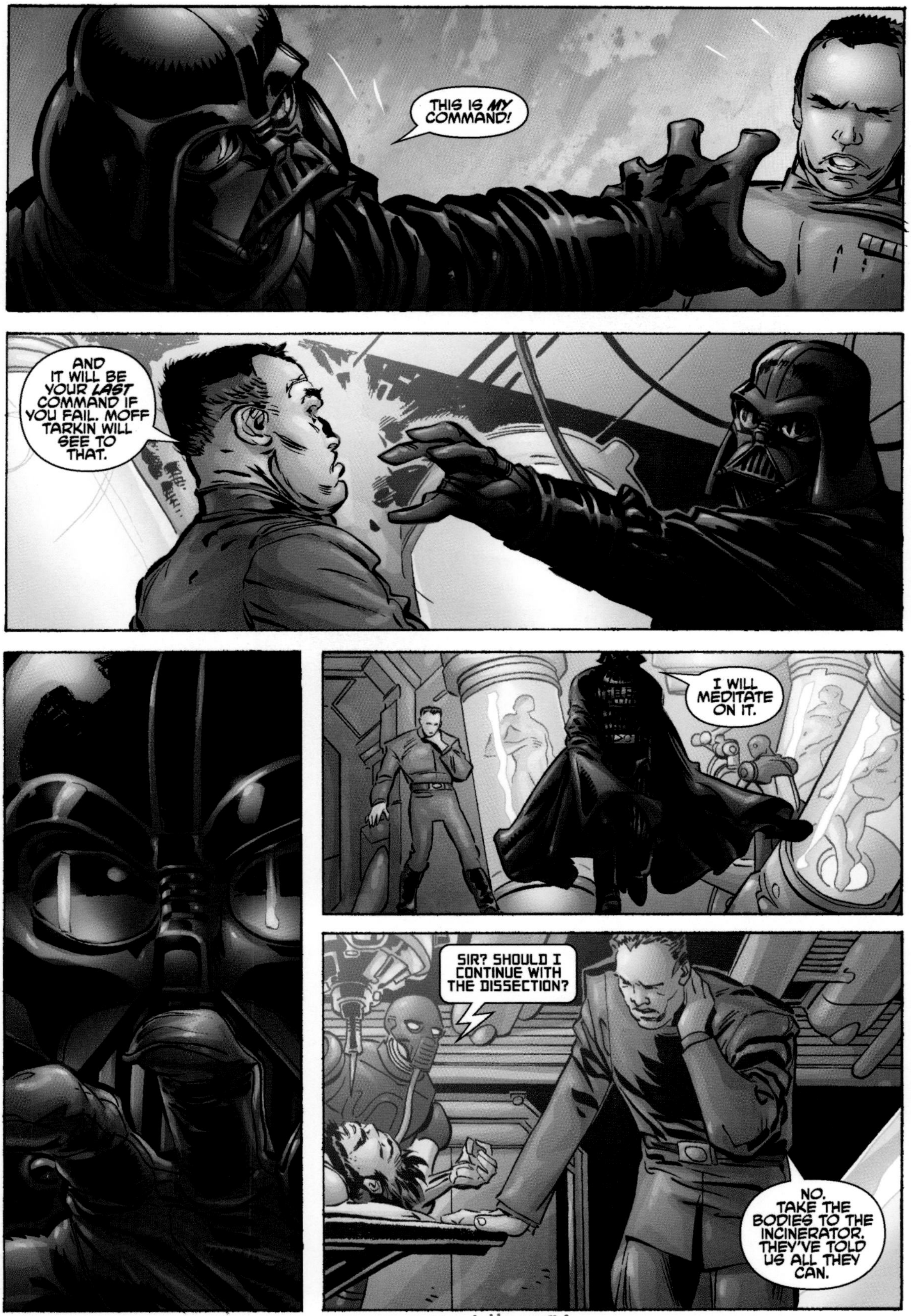
THIS IS MY COMMAND!
AND IT WILL BE YOUR LAST COMMAND IF YOU FAIL. MOFF TARKIN WILL SEE TO THAT.
I WILL MEDITATE ON IT.
SIR? SHOULD I CONTINUE WITH THE DISSECTION?
NO. TAKE THE BODIES TO THE INCINERATOR. THEY'VE TOLD US ALL THEY CAN.

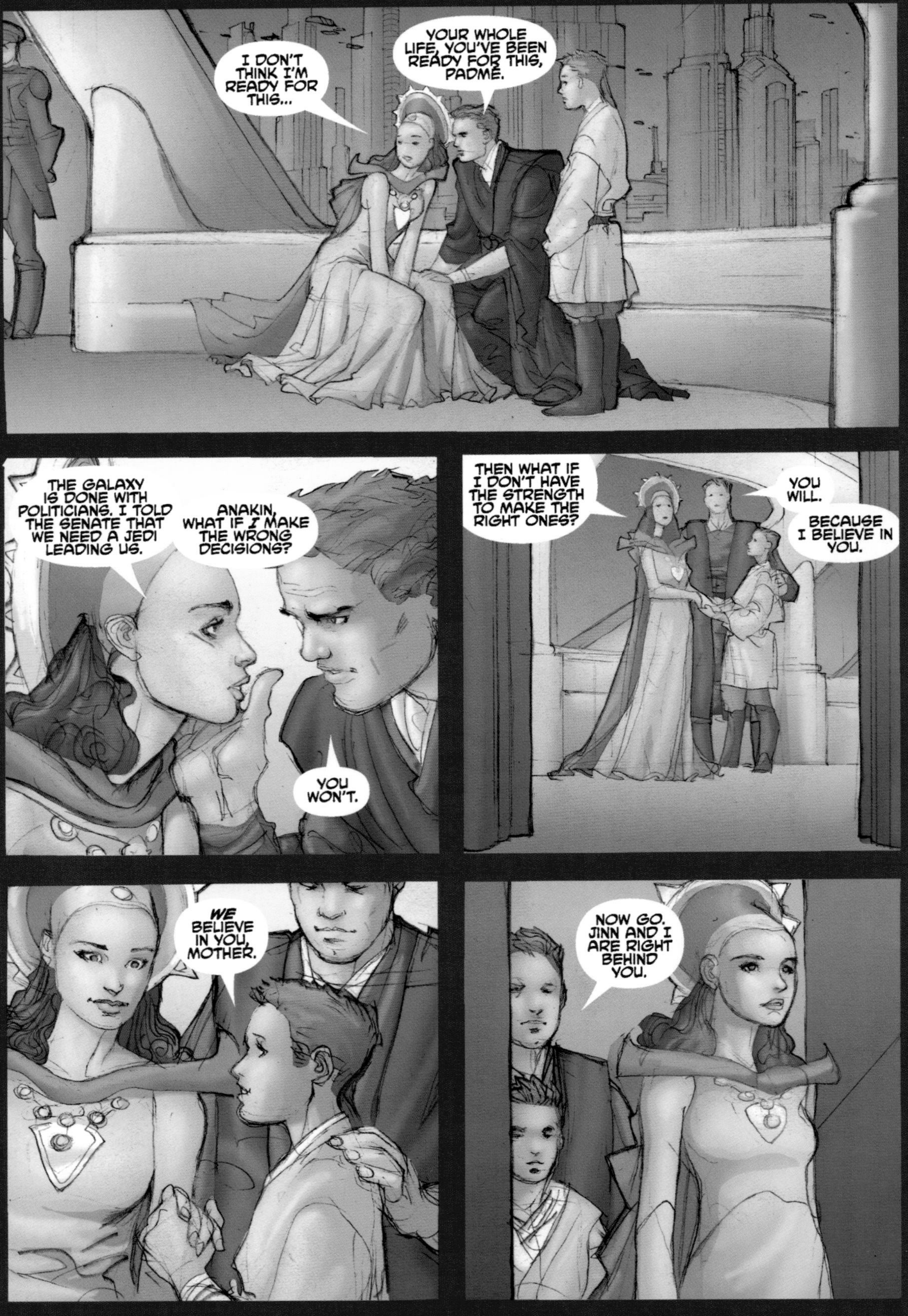
I DON'T THINK I'M READY FOR THIS...
YOUR WHOLE LIFE, YOU'VE BEEN READY FOR THIS, PADMÉ.
THE GALAXY IS DONE WITH POLITICIANS. I TOLD THE SENATE THAT WE NEED A JEDI LEADING US.
ANAKIN, WHAT IF *I* MAKE THE WRONG DECISIONS?
YOU WON'T.
THEN WHAT IF I DON'T HAVE THE STRENGTH TO MAKE THE RIGHT ONES?
YOU WILL.
BECAUSE I BELIEVE IN YOU.
WE BELIEVE IN YOU, MOTHER.
NOW GO. JINN AND I ARE RIGHT BEHIND YOU.

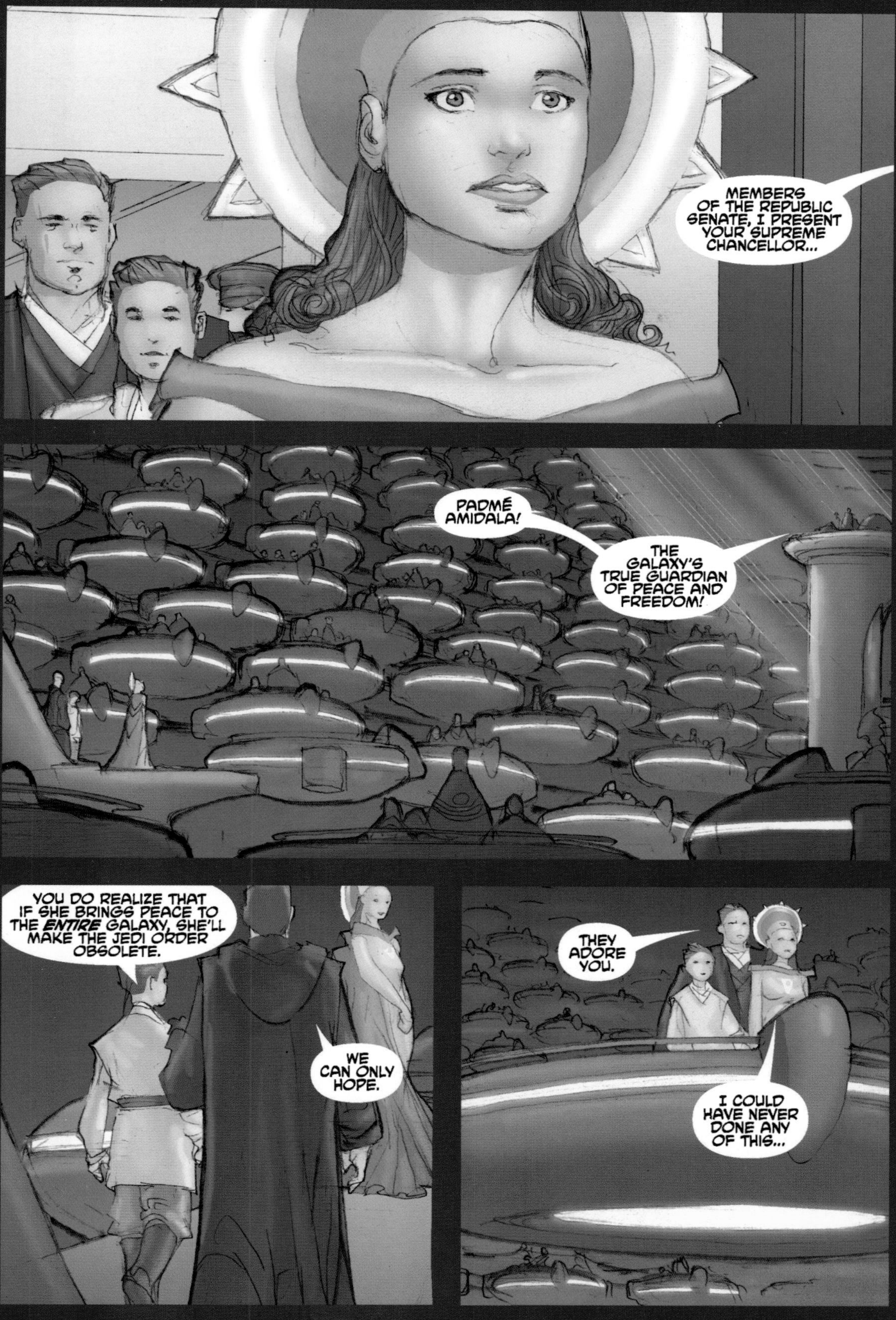
MEMBERS OF THE REPUBLIC SENATE, I PRESENT YOUR SUPREME CHANCELLOR...
PADMÉ AMIDALA!
THE GALAXY'S TRUE GUARDIAN OF PEACE AND FREEDOM!
YOU DO REALIZE THAT IF SHE BRINGS PEACE TO THE *ENTIRE* GALAXY, SHE'LL MAKE THE JEDI ORDER OBSOLETE.
WE CAN ONLY HOPE.
THEY ADORE YOU.
I COULD HAVE NEVER DONE ANY OF THIS...

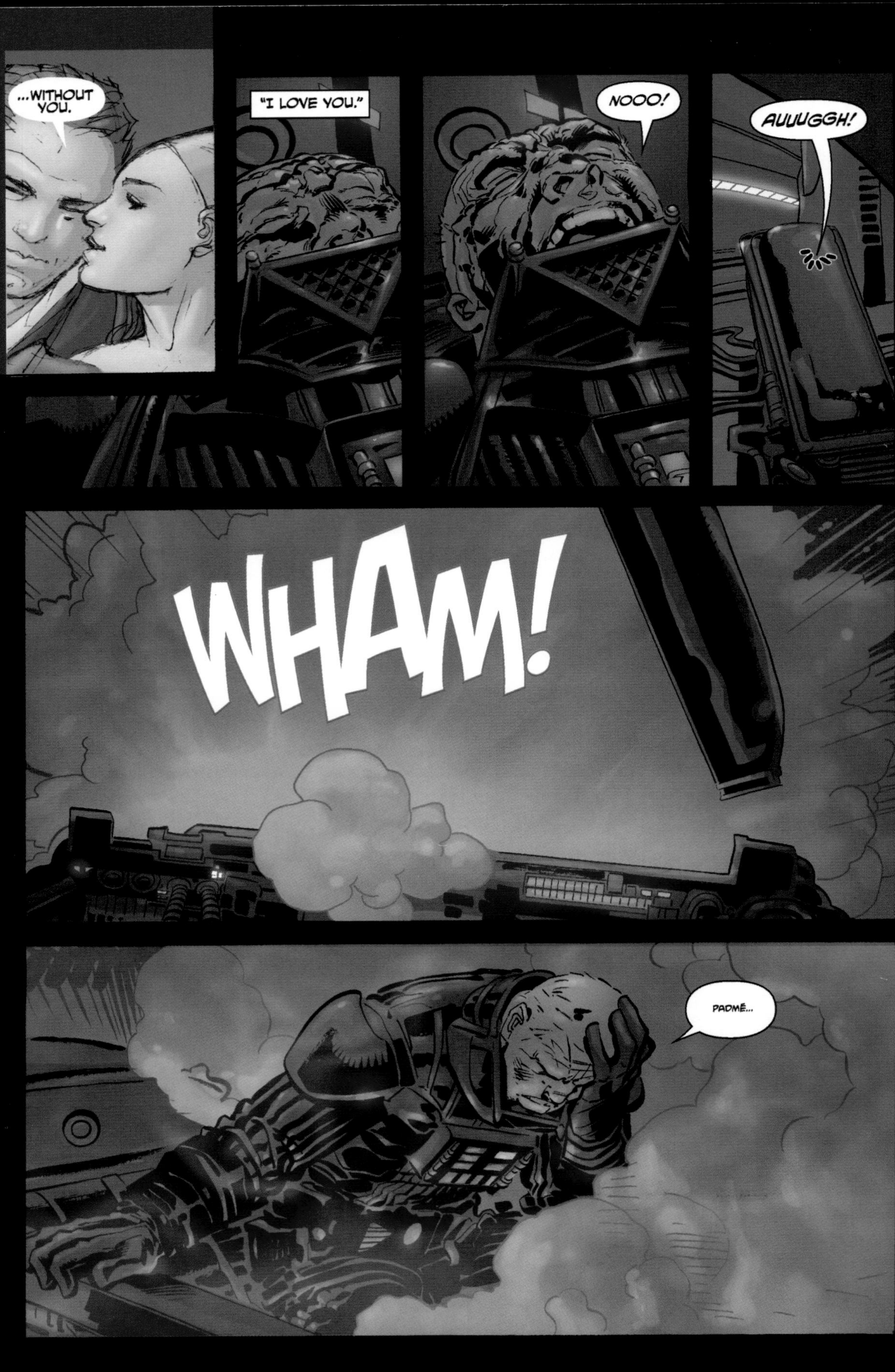
...WITHOUT YOU.
"I LOVE YOU."
NOOO!
AUUUGGH!
WHAM!
PADMÉ...

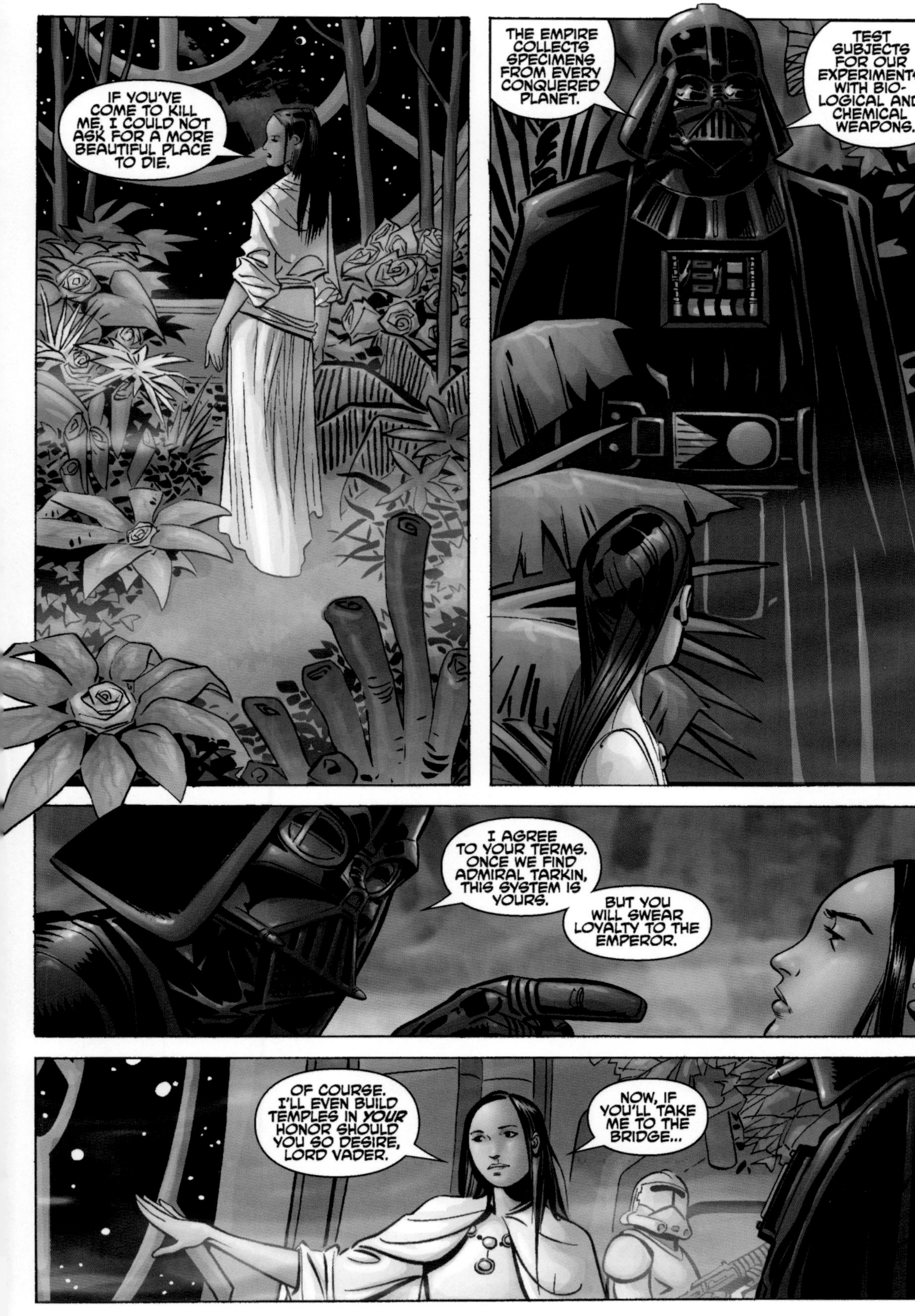
IF YOU'VE COME TO KILL ME, I COULD NOT ASK FOR A MORE BEAUTIFUL PLACE TO DIE.
THE EMPIRE COLLECTS SPECIMENS FROM EVERY CONQUERED PLANET.
TEST SUBJECTS FOR OUR EXPERIMENTS WITH BIO-LOGICAL AND CHEMICAL WEAPONS.
I AGREE TO YOUR TERMS. ONCE WE FIND ADMIRAL TARKIN, THIS SYSTEM IS YOURS.
BUT YOU WILL SWEAR LOYALTY TO THE EMPEROR.
OF COURSE. I'LL EVEN BUILD TEMPLES IN *YOUR* HONOR SHOULD YOU SO DESIRE, LORD VADER.
NOW, IF YOU'LL TAKE ME TO THE BRIDGE...

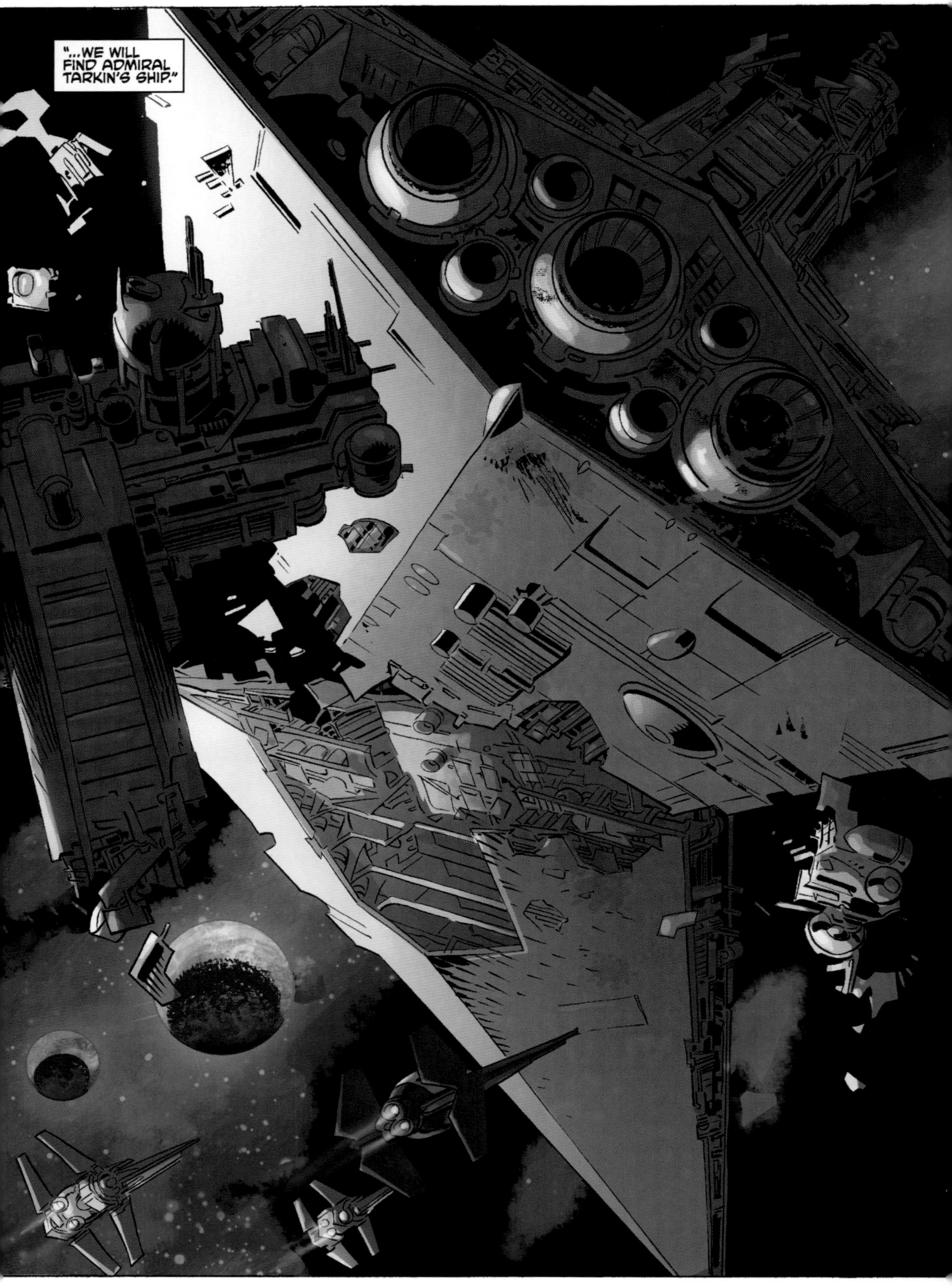
"...WE WILL FIND ADMIRAL TARKIN'S SHIP."

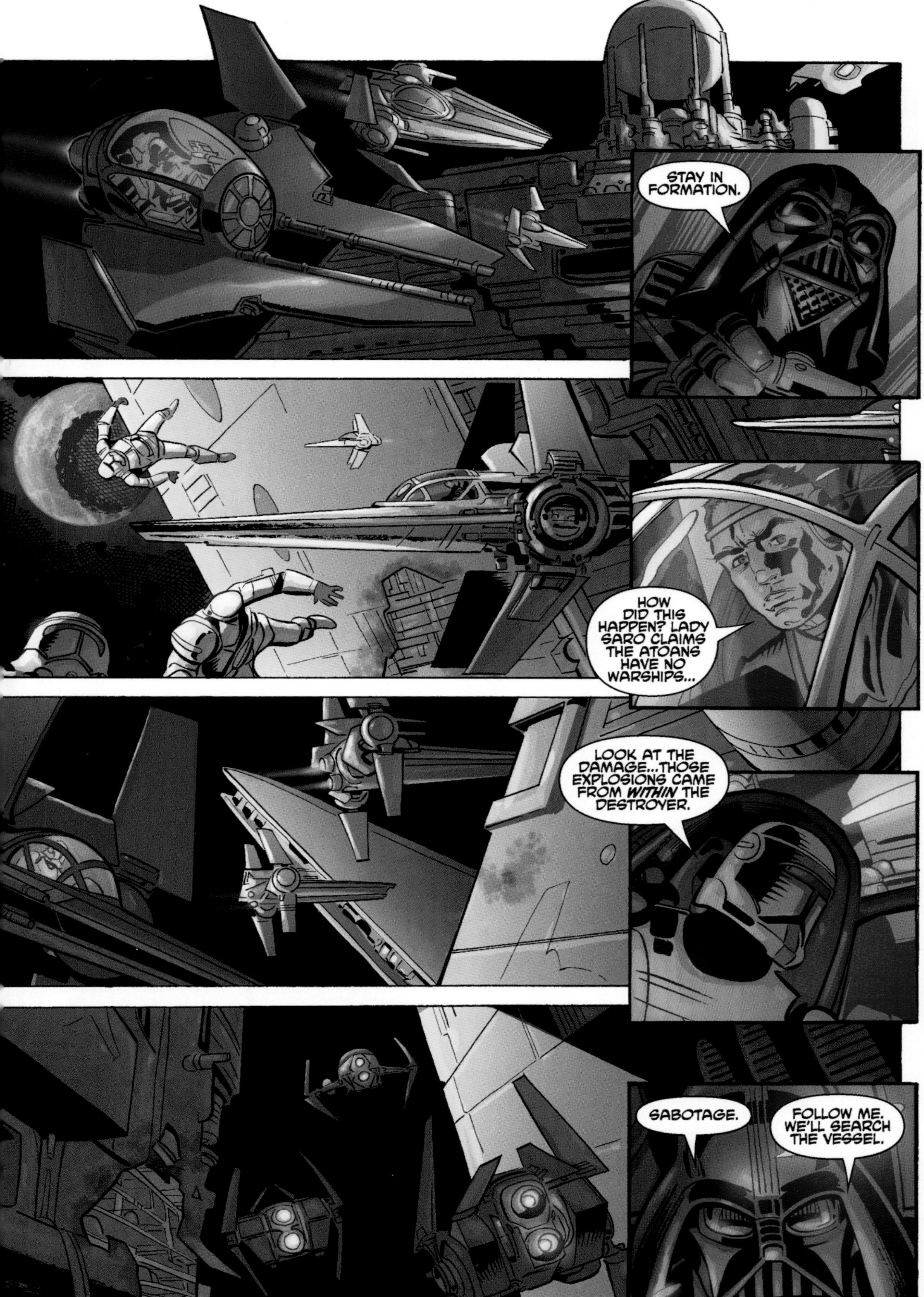
STAY IN FORMATION.
HOW DID THIS HAPPEN? LADY SARO CLAIMS THE ATOANS HAVE NO WARSHIPS...
LOOK AT THE DAMAGE...THOSE EXPLOSIONS CAME FROM *WITHIN* THE DESTROYER.
SABOTAGE.
FOLLOW ME. WE'LL SEARCH THE VESSEL.

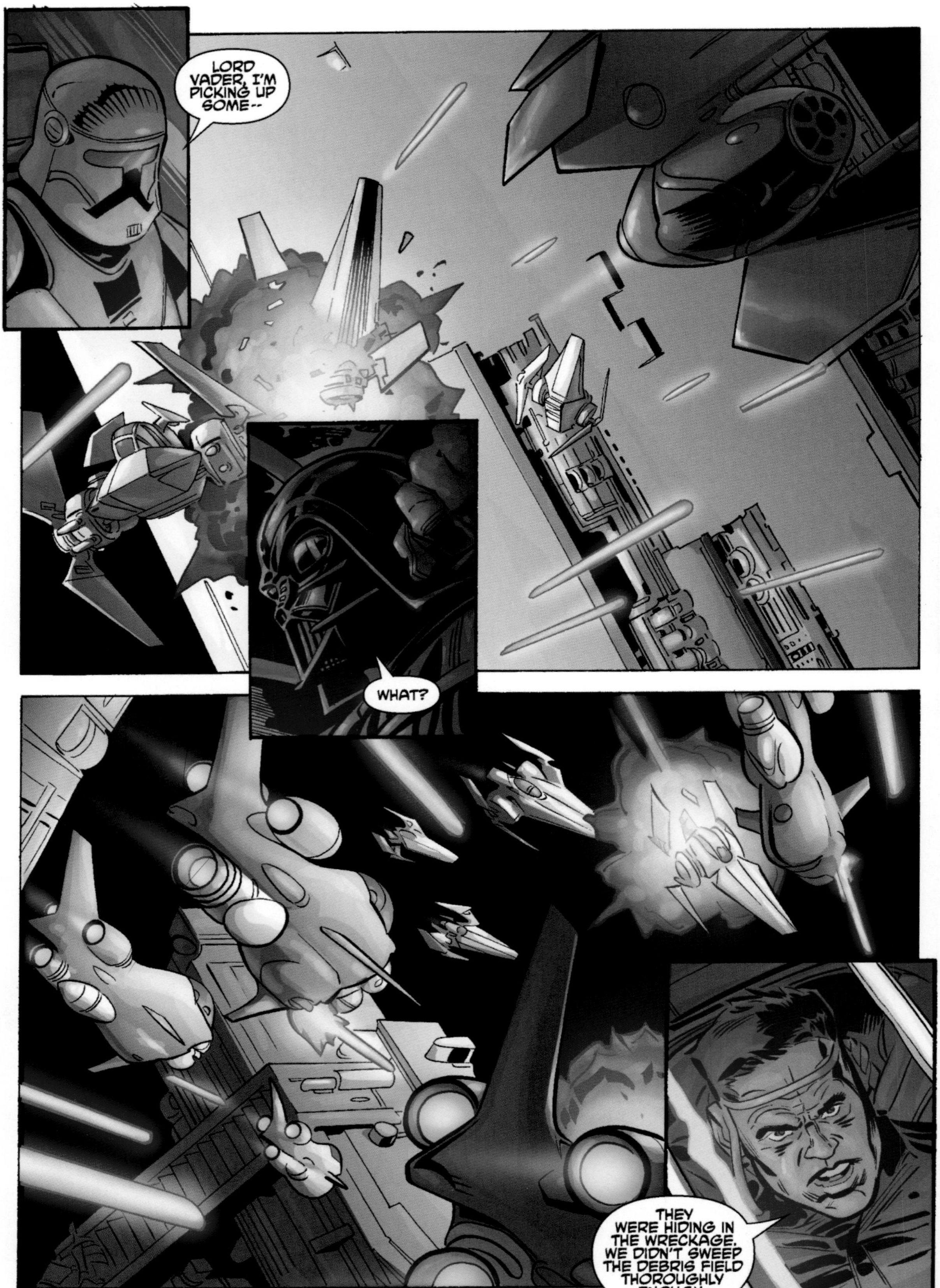
LORD VADER, I'M PICKING UP SOME--
WHAT?
THEY WERE HIDING IN THE WRECKAGE. WE DIDN'T SWEEP THE DEBRIS FIELD THOROUGHLY ENOUGH.

MOVE INTO ATTACK POSITIONS.

IGN'XENG! IGN'XENG! IGN'XENG!

VVVVVV'GGH!!

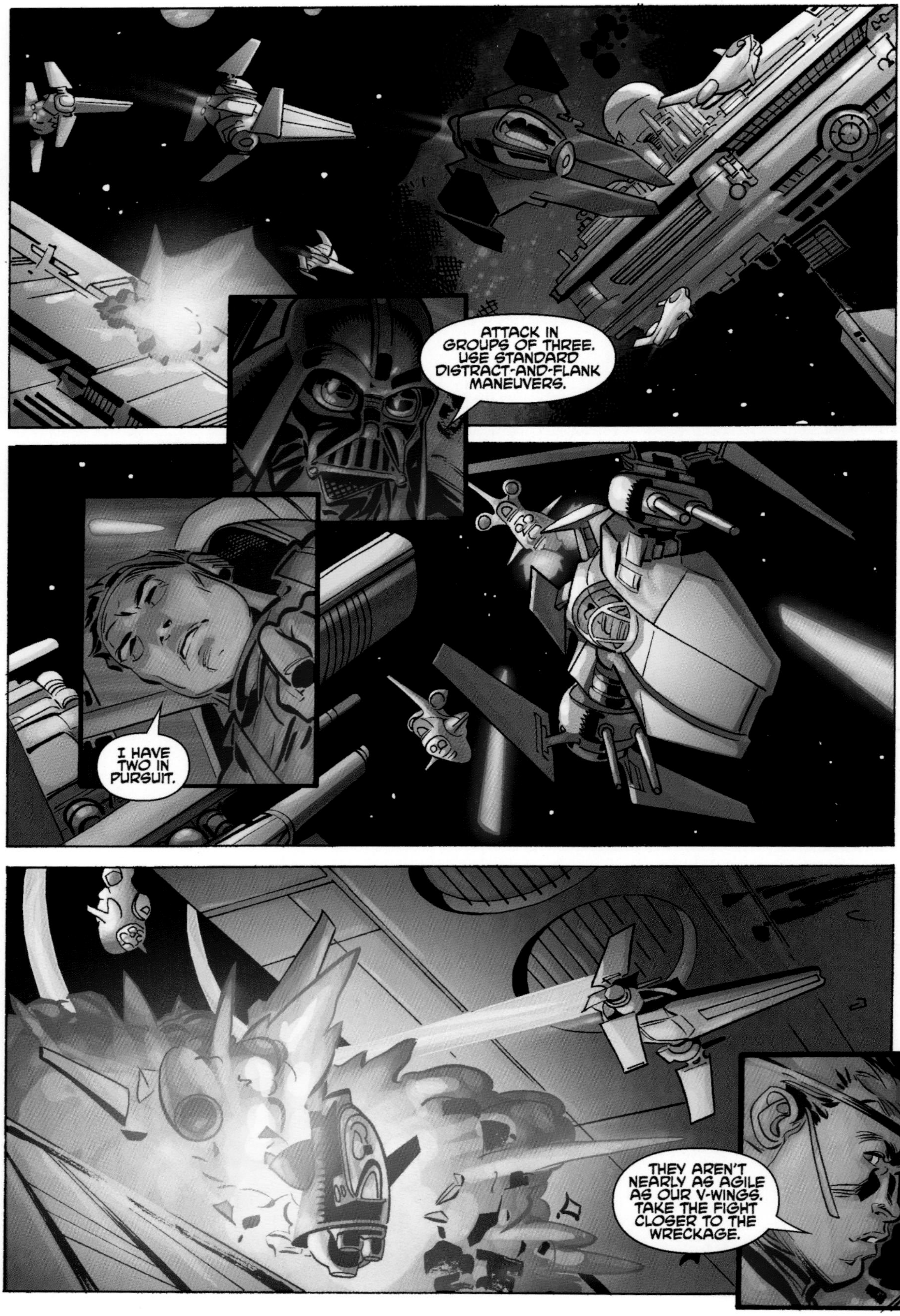
ATTACK IN GROUPS OF THREE. USE STANDARD DISTRACT-AND-FLANK MANEUVERS.
I HAVE TWO IN PURSUIT.
THEY AREN'T NEARLY AS AGILE AS OUR V-WINGS. TAKE THE FIGHT CLOSER TO THE WRECKAGE.

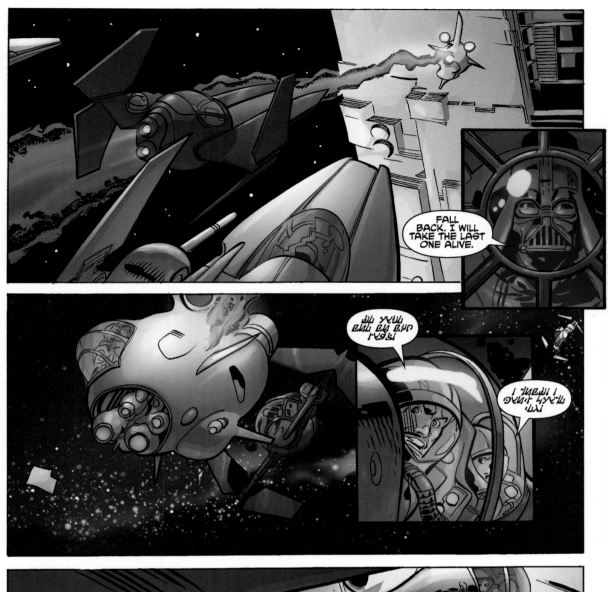

FALL BACK. I WILL TAKE THE LAST ONE ALIVE.

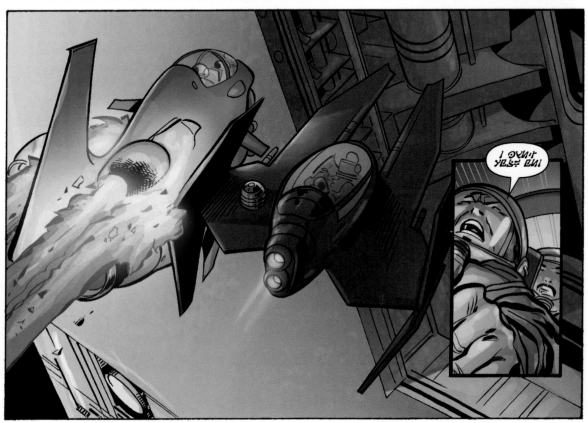

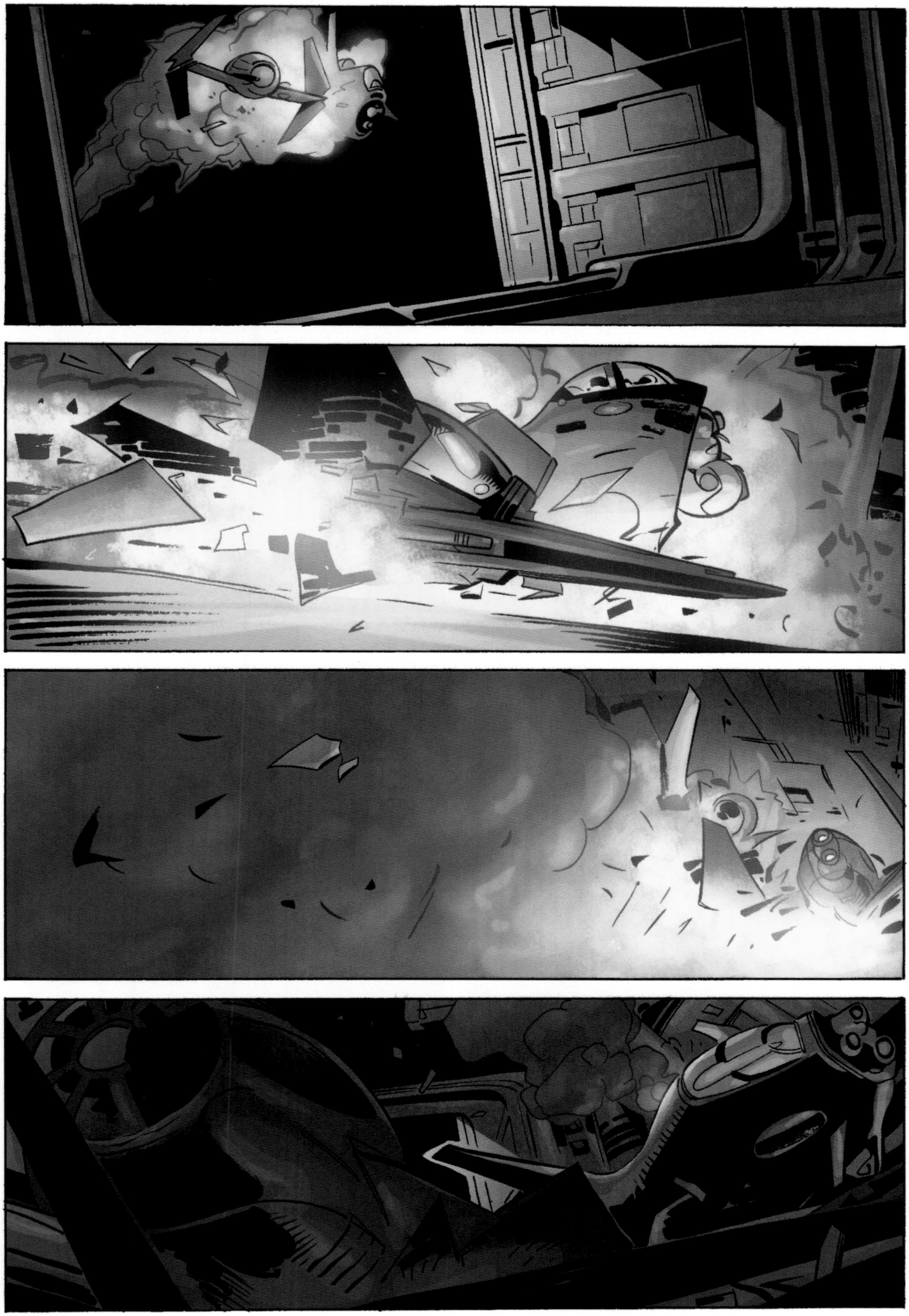

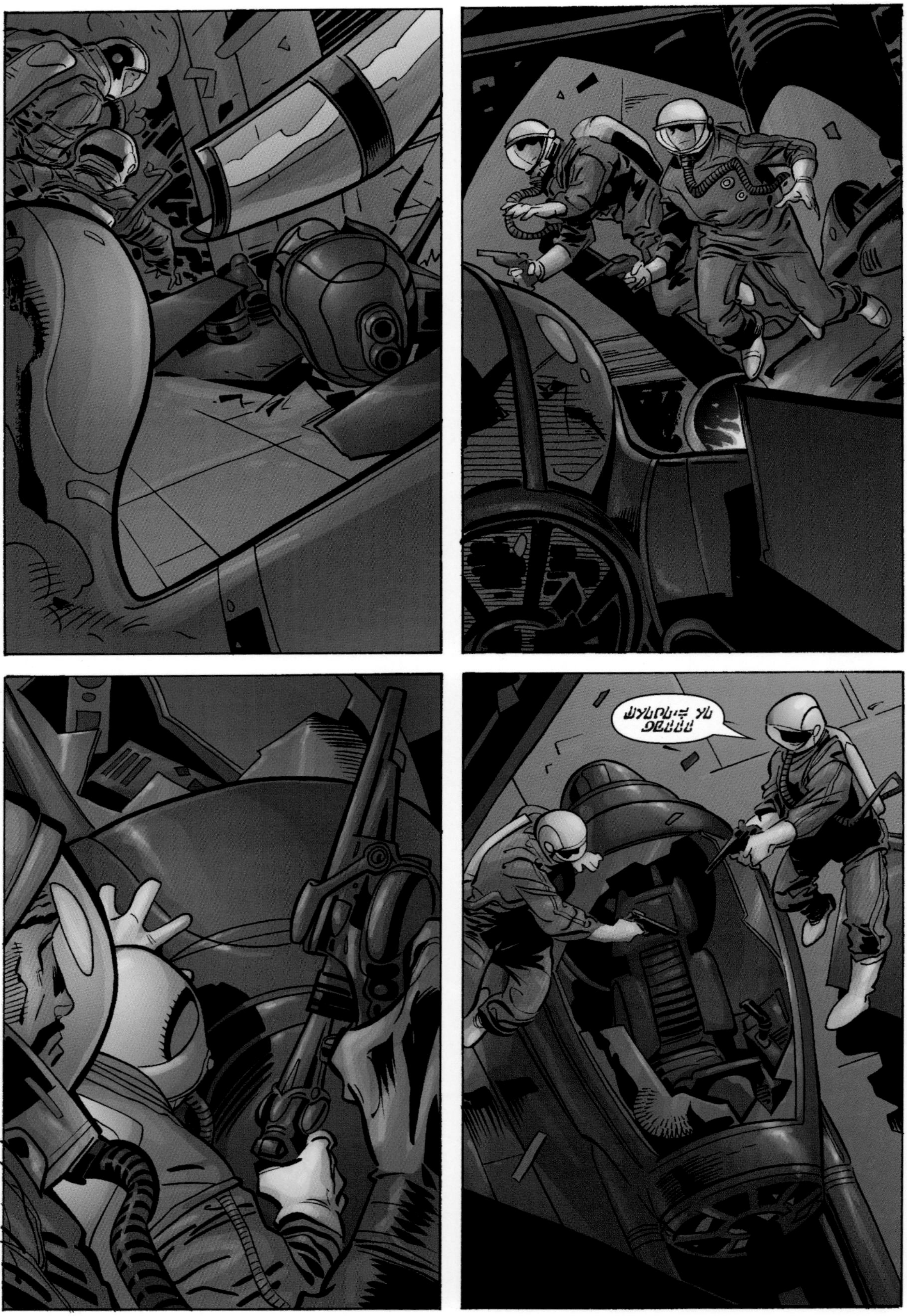

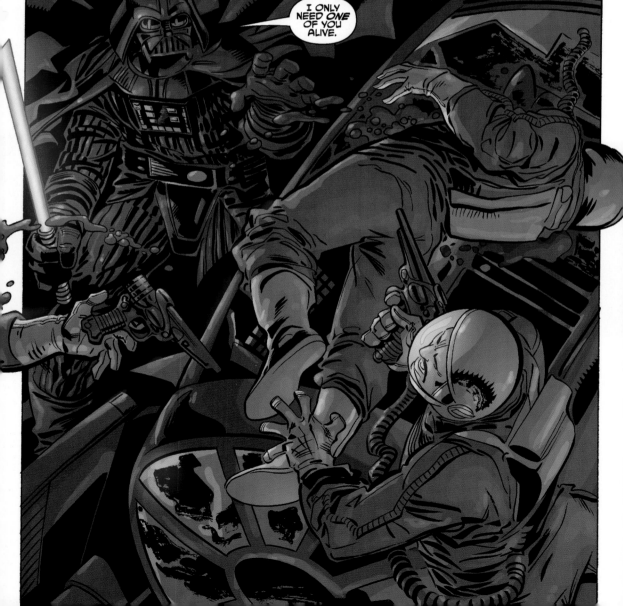

I ONLY NEED *ONE* OF YOU ALIVE.

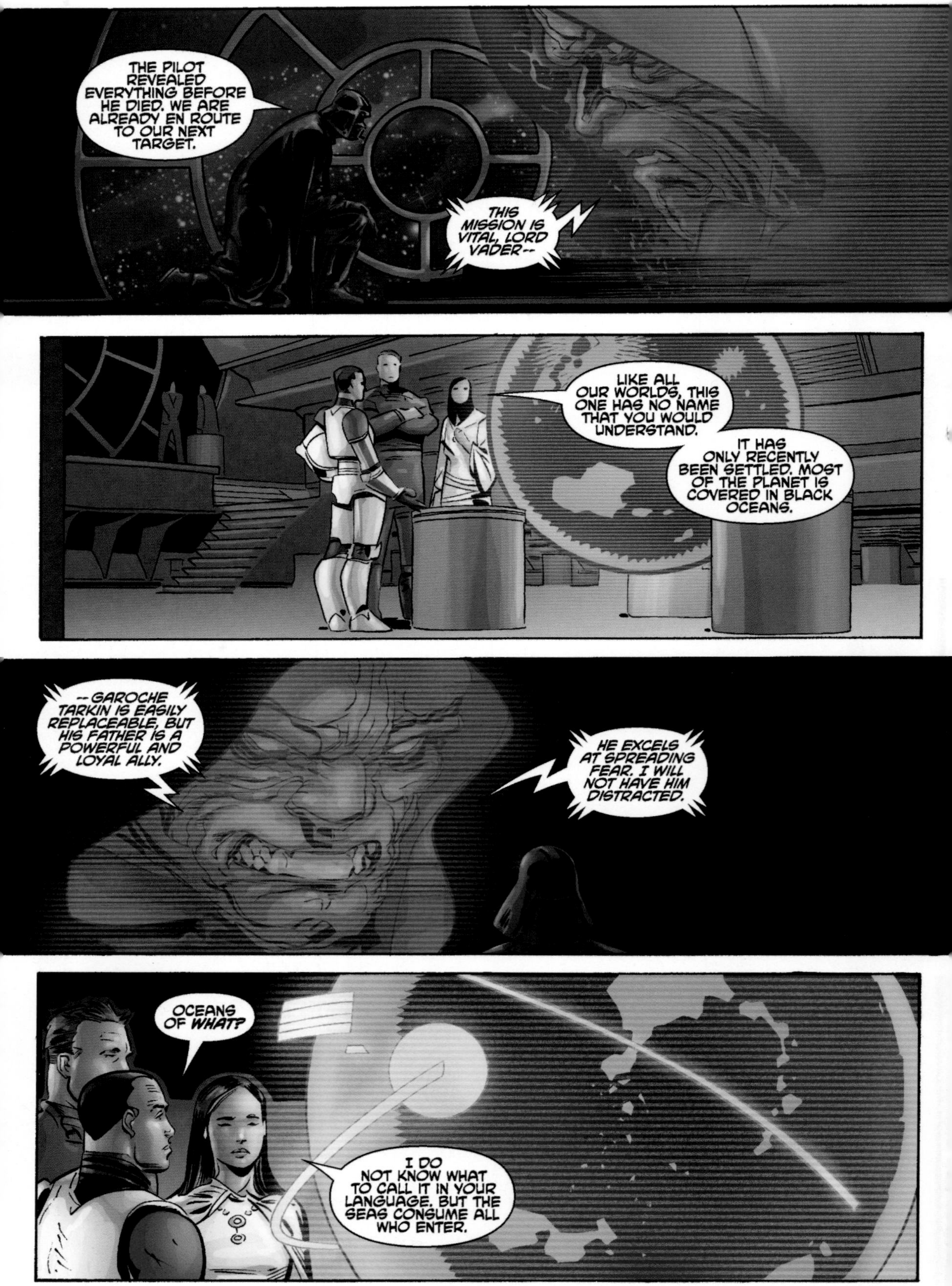
THE PILOT REVEALED EVERYTHING BEFORE HE DIED. WE ARE ALREADY EN ROUTE TO OUR NEXT TARGET.
THIS MISSION IS VITAL, LORD VADER--
LIKE ALL OUR WORLDS, THIS ONE HAS NO NAME THAT YOU WOULD UNDERSTAND.
IT HAS ONLY RECENTLY BEEN SETTLED. MOST OF THE PLANET IS COVERED IN BLACK OCEANS.
--GAROCHE TARKIN IS EASILY REPLACEABLE, BUT HIS FATHER IS A POWERFUL AND LOYAL ALLY.
HE EXCELS AT SPREADING FEAR. I WILL NOT HAVE HIM DISTRACTED.
OCEANS OF *WHAT?*
I DO NOT KNOW WHAT TO CALL IT IN YOUR LANGUAGE. BUT THE SEAS CONSUME ALL WHO ENTER.

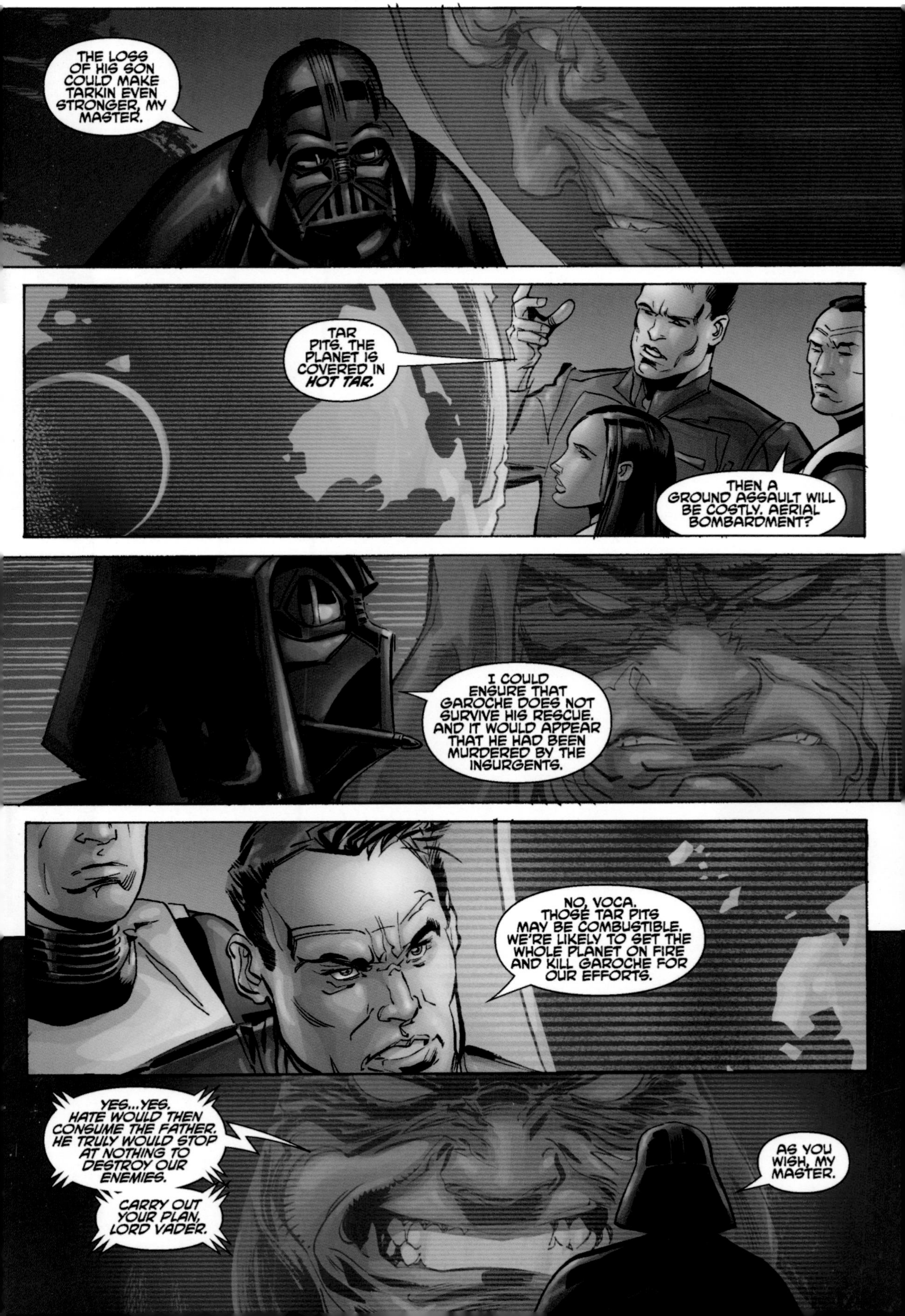
THE LOSS OF HIS SON COULD MAKE TARKIN EVEN STRONGER, MY MASTER.
TAR PITS. THE PLANET IS COVERED IN *HOT TAR.*
THEN A GROUND ASSAULT WILL BE COSTLY. AERIAL BOMBARDMENT?
I COULD ENSURE THAT GAROCHE DOES NOT SURVIVE HIS RESCUE. AND IT WOULD APPEAR THAT HE HAD BEEN MURDERED BY THE INSURGENTS.
NO, VOCA. THOSE TAR PITS MAY BE COMBUSTIBLE. WE'RE LIKELY TO SET THE WHOLE PLANET ON FIRE AND KILL GAROCHE FOR OUR EFFORTS.
YES...YES. HATE WOULD THEN CONSUME THE FATHER. HE TRULY WOULD STOP AT NOTHING TO DESTROY OUR ENEMIES.
CARRY OUT YOUR PLAN, LORD VADER.
AS YOU WISH, MY MASTER.

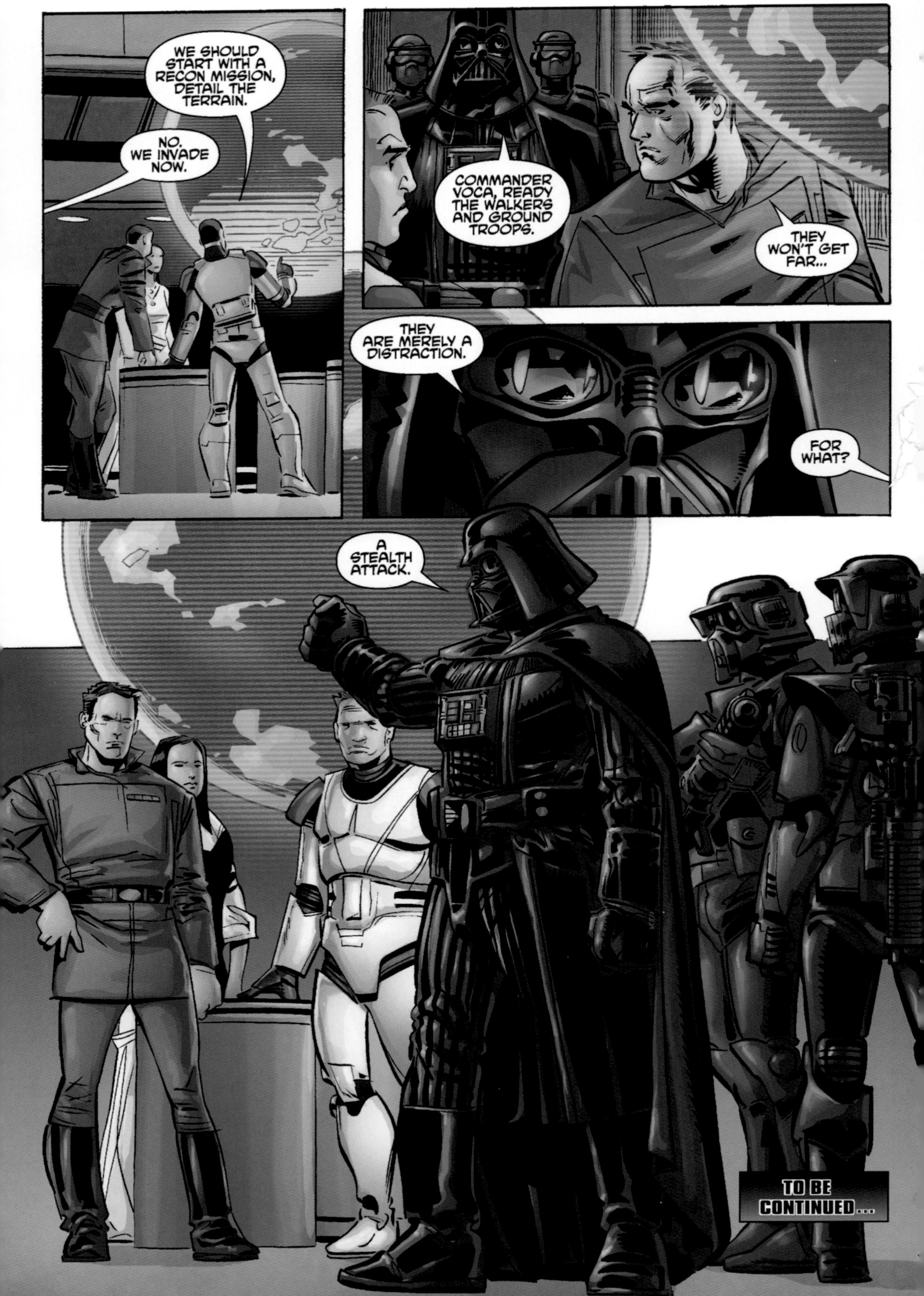
WE SHOULD START WITH A RECON MISSION, DETAIL THE TERRAIN.
NO. WE INVADE NOW.
COMMANDER VOCA, READY THE WALKERS AND GROUND TROOPS.
THEY WON'T GET FAR...
THEY ARE MERELY A DISTRACTION.
FOR WHAT?
A STEALTH ATTACK.
TO BE CONTINUED...